the bea

Well known for its history of secret passages,

pirates and their contraband,

what modern day secrets might this

quaint seaside village hold?

Certainly, one you have never come across
before!

Chapter 1

The wind whirled its way over the cobbles of the curling Main Street, causing the chimes over the general store door to tinkle.

At least that's how it might have been perceived by the living, the dead knew better.

Those who lingered in this little fishing village after their demise whether violent, vicious or quietly in their beds, recognised that mischievous sound – Belle!

What had the little 'monkey' been up to now?

There was no doubt some little trick was afoot, whether it be against some holiday visitor, local villager, or indeed against one of their number, the 'Departed Spirits' or the 'Desperates'. Sounds so much better than 'ghosts', don't you think?

Technically speaking of course, they hadn't departed in the real sense of the word because they were still here but the dead don't tend to split hairs; everything to them is black or white!

Not to Belle, she was the most colourful little 'desperate' you could ever meet, not that most people will of course, if you know what I mean; yet Belle loved life so, even if that meant living it in death.

She enjoyed herself to the full and made the most of being invisible, causing havoc to the living at every opportunity. Although she was never malicious, she could be irritating if her tricks caused real disruption to someone's everyday routine, not to mention finances.

Like the time she played the trick on the couple from London who were staying in the - 'Village View' cottage up on the hillside: -

Nice young couple but a bit out of their depth and not very streetwise when it came to managing anything other than the hustle and bustle of their working lives in the city.
Gavin and Chloe were just settling in and starting to appreciate the peace and quiet when Belle chose to have a little fun with them.

She chose a day when the weather was inclement - a sea fret to those in the know.

The townies were preparing to go off to Whitby for the day to explore, safer than staying here and tackling the cliffs in this weather.

It was probably a bad idea to venture outside in only a pair of Y Fronts anyway, but there was nothing wrong with Gavin's logic that if he couldn't see his hand in front of him, then others wouldn't be able to see his state of undress as he reached for his walking boots from the rack outside the door.

The rack seemed much further away than when Chloe had insisted, they take advantage of using it and not having to trail mud through the little house.

As he stood on the pavement shivering, his slightly addled brain (influenced by last night's indulgence at the Smugglers inn) started to register that there was only one pair of boots resting on the rack and they weren't his!

'Chloe' yelled Gavin at the top of his voice, obviously convinced that the shroud of cloud surrounding him had the power to conceal sound as well as sight from anyone within hearing distance: -

'Chloe have you taken my boots inside?'

'What?' came the indelicate reply from a voice standing next to him on the small pavement, this one dressed in a see-through negligée.

Obviously, one of the things they had in common was their logic pertaining to sea mist!

Before Gavin could repeat his inquiry there was a loud bang and a sharp click, followed by the slow realisation that the door had been blown shut.

It must have been a freak gust of wind for although the weather was damp, cold and misty, wind had not appeared to be an issue so far today.

'Oh no,' came the involuntary shivering shout from the almost naked blue Gavin who had by now started dancing, trying to keep warm.

'Don't worry - I made sure the latch was off,' Chloe's warm sweet voice reassured him, (She had obviously missed the clicking noise!)

Only when she tried the door, which resolutely refused to open, did she join him in absolute hysteria as to the dawning horror of their situation.

Despite the mist Chloe could see the accusatory expression starting to form on the face in front of her, 'There's bound to be someone in one of the other cottages,' she forced, hoping she sounded believable, 'and they'll let us use the phone or they might have a spare key, come on'

'Are you completely mad? We are both nearly as naked as the day we were born! How can we go knocking on someone else's door? We need to think!'

They both became aware of a tinkling sound around them; the shop was open and it had customers! That actually made their predicament seem worse somehow, as they were hardly in a position to descend the hill: - that would be worse than facing the neighbours.

Their conversation from the previous evening suddenly dawned on them, they had been elated that there were no neighbours to disturb, as they had noisily made their way back from the local hostelry.

Chloe began to cry and Gavin, distressed by the sound, decided to take his anger out on the unyielding door, banging his fists with all his might.

Click...

Unbelievably the door swung open. Their agony was over.

They didn't hang around to question it, or the whereabouts of Gavin's boots: - they literally threw themselves inside seeking warmth and safety.

Later they would question how that could possibly have happened, and would inform the owner of the cottage that the lock was unreliable and needed changing.

As I said before, Belle is not malicious just irritating, and sometimes expensive, but Belle is never one to take a joke too far!

Chapter 2

Belle's story is a strange one and quite possibly one you have never heard before.

I know you are curious so I will explain how this beautiful little mischief maker ended up in a small fishing village on the east coast of Yorkshire, growing up in spirit without the company of anyone who knew her.

There was little of her to know really - that's the main reason - and Belle knew very little and understood less herself.

The travel company considered it to be one of the worst possible ends to a school trip that they had ever experienced but the fact that it had involved an adult and not one of the children was seen by some as a blessing.

Class 6 had been having a lovely time playing on the sand when it was suggested that they might want to go for a walk up the Main Street or on the grassy hillside above them that led down to Gobble Hole further up the coastline.

Many dainty little girls in pretty beach outfits chose the former.

The more blood thirsty adventure seeking boys liked the sound of the latter, noisily wondering how it had got its name.

Laughter rang out as the class comedian explained the cold dark cave just above the water line was where the villagers stored their Turkeys in the days before Christmas when they couldn't get them in their freezers.

Even their teacher, who was trying hard to think of a reason to stay on the beach sunbathing, had to laugh at the lad's quick thinking.

Claire usually enjoyed the class trips but she felt really out of sorts today.

She could have put the upset stomach and queasiness down to the coach journey over the moors but Claire remembered how she'd felt this morning when she woke up and that she had been in two minds whether to ring in sick.

She had listened to her late mother's voice coming from deep inside her, 'you can't let them down on a day like today and the break will do you good'.

Claire's mum had often given good advice whilst alive - no reason to argue with her- especially now she didn't always have to follow it!

It was lovely that her mum could still give orders really and Claire was usually very grateful for the advice.

Today would turn out to be different.

The short straw of accompanying the climbers up the hillside was mainly given to Claire because of her ability to manage the more boisterous of her class who had chosen this course rather than the retail or historical experience of the village.

If she had confided in her colleagues about how she was feeling then they would have insisted she stay and rest with the less strenuous faction of their party, but she didn't.

Gobble hole had not gained its name as previously suggested - it went back to a time long before the villagers could have afforded turkey as their main course at any time of year, least of all Christmas.

The coastal outline had changed over the years, the water wearing down the bottom of the cliff edge slowly but persistently over the centuries.

Some of the damage was only visible from the water and lead to overhangs of grass along the cliff top. Green curtains of uneven lengths drawn haphazardly over the cliff's edge obscuring the imminent danger beneath.

The fishermen were aware as they made their way back with their haul and would warn their families of the dangers of going near the edge of the cliff but visitors were very few and far between in those days.

What was less obvious to the naked eye was the damage the cliff was undergoing on
the inside, especially the fabric closest to the cliff walls. The outside surfaces suffered the relentless battering of the turbulent sea like the skin of a drum taking a constant beating.

Meantime in places the inside was starting to crumble as if surrendering rather than waiting to be taken prisoner by nature itself.

The grass carpet that covered any sign of the inner decay, dipped and bowed more precariously the closer one got to the edge but concealed its secret admirably from wandering boots.

That is until the strain became too much and holes appeared - only ever under the pressure of at least 180 lbs (approx.80kgs) and exactly the size of an average cliff walker carrying a rucksack.

Fortunately, most victims who were 'gobbled' in this fashion were found before too much damage had taken place and were rescued, those who weren't are not for now but may appear in a future novel!

The Health and Safety Executive (local branch) were first founded and then alerted to the situation and excavation was ordered; however, common sense prevailed once a natural cave deep within the rock revealed itself and the diggers were sent packing.

Gobble hole was christened and became a new source of revenue for the village, bringing visitors from far and wide - well from the rest of Yorkshire at least but enough to put this very small picturesque village on the map!

Meanwhile back on the hillside the pressure of keeping several small unqualified rock climbers under control was starting to create an issue for Claire.

The sound of her own voice getting louder and more urgent in its commands to 'be careful' confirmed that staying aloft was a bad idea and she should allow the children to descend into the cave which is what they were craving.

She longed to be back on the beach herself as she was aware of the overwhelming need to sit down and have a cold drink and maybe take some painkillers for the griping pain in her insides.

How to manage that though whilst making sure those at the front and back were all safe?

Where was the other adult who had been nominated to accompany her? Surely pulling on slacks and a T-shirt over trunks didn't take that long.

Claire would not admit to herself that she should have listened to her mother urging her to wait for him, mainly because she just wanted to get this over with and return to the sunbathing.

Afterwards Claire wasn't sure if she slipped, was pushed or if she just fainted but hitting the top side of the cave with a bang and sliding down the curving walls and landing in a blood splattered heap at the bottom was still a vivid memory.

Her second memory was waking in a hospital bed being told she had only suffered minor scratches and severe bruising but had lost the baby she hadn't known she was carrying.

Chapter 3

Something felt very different, whilst still experiencing the dark and moist feeling that was usual, there was a sense of freedom that was much more than the lack of restriction recently endured.

There was light both inside and out (past the darkness) and the desire to move and relish the freedom one had been unexpectedly given, was undeniable.

Despite sounds around there was a sense of detachment and curiosity. The desire to move forward toward the outer light became undeniable.

There had been sounds before, always muffled, but suddenly everything exploded into being, more sensed than seen or heard.

Of course, 'ns' 'now spiritual' was incorporated in what one could 'see', obvious really!

It would take time but eventually 'sense' would be made of everything that was around now.

Learning would come from exploring, listening and watching and the realisation that there was no need to hide - no one else was aware - freedom meant that you could have anything or everything.

Only those working on a spiritual level would be able to 'sense' presence.

This was Belle's beginning - a point of light set free in a relentlessly dark cave - a creation of circumstance and of movement. An overwhelming desire for experience without restriction or boundary.

This led to the entity's unique future circumstance and existence as one of the local 'departed'. Technically there had never been an existence so there couldn't really have been a departure in the way the others had, but that didn't seem to matter.

As said before, only the living appear to be concerned by accuracy in what those who have passed, see as unnecessary detail.

I can't explain the strength of spirit and determination showed by this miraculous product of what most would call tragic circumstances.

I can, however, outline how it actually became known and accepted as Belle by the other unseen inhabitants of the village.

The beautiful, minuscule point of light darted this way and that down alleyways that twisted and turned the entire length of the hillside (more of that later).

How wonderful it was to float high over things and dip low amongst them, totally undisturbed.

There was a lovely light tinkling sound that appeared to happen every time a collision was avoided and the other solid participant looked around them in confusion - no idea as to what had ethereally disturbed them.

Then it happened - a vision appeared - not from nowhere obviously - it had always been on the front of the large Victorian book, but it had not always been on show in the front window of the local book shop.

The most beautiful thing ever seen.

If it was possible to be anything you wanted to be then this was it - a small figure in a pretty dress with blue eyes blonde hair and ringlets.

Projection it appeared was a natural progression of being 'light.'

How wonderful to be whatever you imagined yourself to be and then show that to others, even if others only included those who also 'lived' in the 'twilight' rather than in one of the quaint cottages around them. It was they who gave her the name Belle because of the tinkling sound of her laughter which sounded like a bell - did you guess?

I added the 'e' because although the two may have sounded alike, there was nothing hard or shrill about Belle.

Ah yes, 'the others' what about them?

Chapter 4

The old fishing village climbed from the shore to the cliff top more by accident than by design.

It was the product of necessary housing for the farmers turned fishermen in the early days, although housing sounds a rather grand term for the shacks that first appeared around the bay. They were far enough away from the sea but somewhere to sleep within easy reach of their boats early the next day.

The hike up the cliff remains challenging, even today with cobbles, paving stone paths and hand rails, it is not for the fainthearted.

Families that started life at the top of the cliff accepted their menfolk having to struggle up and down the treacherous cliff. They had to supplement their diet of potatoes and the like with the much-needed fish from the bountiful sea.

As the sea battered the cliffs and the bay showed itself to be safe and sheltered, the dwellings grew in number as well as stature, enabling those at the top to join those at the bottom. The village as we know it today was formed.

The complexity of building on this terrain produced twists and turns that were then used by the villagers to protect their livelihood which evolved from the natural offerings of the sea to the more lucrative – shipwrecks of course!

You will not hear here any nasty rumour that the ships were 'lured' onto the rocks deliberately but it has to be said that help provided by those nearest at hand during the disaster, whether natural or not, was for themselves and not shared with the taxman.

It has since been said that the old passageways used within the building of their homes meant that a bale of silk could pass from the bottom of the village to the top without leaving the inside of the houses.

Belle just loved the uneven narrow streets that climbed the hillside and she spent lots of time weaving in and out of the 'hidden' spaces inside the dwellings that had saved many from the pressgangs and the inland revenue over the years.

She had lots of fun and obviously didn't know any different so neither knew nor cared why the twists, turns and holes were there.

Whilst she had no understanding of the latter, she was aware of the others who appeared to exist as she did, undetected by the 'restricted' inhabitants of the area.

That's how she sensed them – they had the freedom she enjoyed, but they certainly didn't 'project' themselves in any flattering way.

They all appeared the same to her and they moved around together. I imagine that scene would have been very frightening to those who were still breathing, if they could see them.

Not to Belle, their existence was just another thing she sensed without having to understand it.

Eavesdropping was something else open to her as a pastime but not as exciting as it may sound because many of the terms used, although they became familiar, meant nothing really.

Stories of pirates, fishwives, hiding from the inland revenue or pressgangs might conjure fear or excitement in some but not in Belle.

Those feelings though, did create different vibrations in those around her, which in turn added to her experience in many ways but was also beyond her understanding.

The memory of any previous existence, or the benefit of friendly advice during this one, might have produced deference to the other departed souls; deference that would allow for their superior knowledge, experience and in some cases obvious suffering that had influenced their life (and death), however she had no such memory.

Everything was just as it was and all was accepted and seen as equal to her, despite her not actually knowing or understanding what that meant. 'Sense' differentiated for her in all things. Her tinkling sound was her signature to those around anything she was involved in and it never altered.

Growling sounds of disapproval or anger often rose from the local grisly shaped apparitions that would have struck horror in the world's strongest inhabitants, if they ever heard them. They had little or no effect on this little miracle of nature.

Belle was totally protected by her innocence and lack of understanding as I believe most of our children are meant to be but sadly often are not.

Her lack of fear and other emotions meant that the others were unable to control her in the way they might have wished to do.

If they found her appearance confusing, who knows?

It was unlikely they had ever confronted the image of a very well to do Victorian child during their lifetime, because most of them were either pirates or men who had been the victims of press gangs returning to their village post death as they were prevented from returning before then.

The latter were the only ones really who were suspicious, taking their mistrust into the afterlife with them.

Any others who remained behind had their own agendas to occupy them which usually had to do with not wanting to leave behind others who were still breathing!

Chapter 5

Whilst Belle mostly spent her time in the open air, travelling at speed and entertaining herself with moving silently and undetected around the village, the more sinister of the 'Desperates' did not.

The main hideout for the brigands in their lifetime had been the 'T'hole in the T'wall'
(the hole in the wall for those of you who are not familiar with the Yorkshire dialect.)

If you are imagining a cosy little snug with a warm open fire, squat away from the cruelty of the waves that often battered the cliff – think again!

It sounds like a pub and indeed as the years passed it was often used as a pub by the villagers but it started life as just that – a hole in the sea wall perfect for storage.

The villagers used the crumbling of the inner cliff to their absolute advantage and in the early days of settlement used nature's refrigeration to keep their fish fresh, safe from the sea water and the sun.

Later as the buildings developed and grew, these holes formed natural cellars for spirits and contraband that came from ships that suffered unfortunate 'accidents' in the surrounding waters.

The stored barrels of rum and brandy especially, made hiding from the revenue men or press gang slightly more endurable during the early days. The secret passage way to the beach was never discovered.

This was mainly because all movement was made in the dark just before the tide came in fully.

The terrain was so treacherous, no sane minded person would contemplate that anyone would risk their life trying to reach that part of the cliff that faced out to sea.

Why would you? As far as could be seen there was no access to anywhere and the tiny strip of sand the pirates used never showed itself in daylight, which was very useful.

As the years passed, rooms appeared above the cellars, naturally forming a meeting place for the sailors to drink and be merry.

Access then was from the village where the other dwellings were slowly being built. It seemed natural that those who made their living from selling the spirits that were eventually legally purchased, would make the home for their family on top.

So, the 'hole' crept upwards and upwards through-out the years, the access being created at the bottom, from the slipway to the sea, for deliveries from the brewery to what became known as 'The Old Jolly Rodger'.

Its outward appearance at the top eventually created the lower of the two corner buildings that stood like bookends holding open the sea view to the six other cottages that occupied the main square of the village.

It all sounds much grander than it actually was, because being at the mercy of the sea and its moods meant the sitting area of the square had to sacrifice any comfort in its seating, relying on stone or metal benches that could withstand the weather.

It meant those wanting to see the ships on the horizon or watch their children playing whilst waiting for their menfolk to finish their business or merry making, needed to be of stalwart proportions. Like the hill, not for the faint hearted!

As the years passed and the inhabitants of the village had access to cars and supermarkets filled with cheap booze the pub like many, closed and the landlord moved away. Very sad!

Not everybody thought so. This is where 'the others' hung out – back where they started all those years ago. They shed no tears (spirits don't cry) for the comfort that this dwelling had lost – they never knew it.

Their eternal plan was to remain in the safety of the gloomy cellars in peace and quiet, venturing out only when they felt the need, fairly sure of their anonymity.

The more suspicious of you may think they helped bring about the early demise of the hostelry and its occupants, having the capacity as they had to intimidate mere human beings.

If Belle wondered why the strange looking creatures who shared her freedom, didn't use it as she did and lingered most of the time in the dark dreary cave, similar to where she started her journey, we will never know.

It didn't matter anyway, occupying different areas and pastimes worked for them and no encroachment from either party meant a peaceful existence for all.

That is until…….

Chapter 6

Not following instructions was one of Jeremy's highly polished skills and though irritating to his bosses in the past, it was probably the main reason he now owned his own successful business.

The estate agent must have been mad telling him there were no suitable properties with a view of the sea for sale here. This fed his belief that most people outside the city of London had no real thirst for work and seemed to see it as a necessary evil and therefore only did the basics.

If the agent had any foresight, he would have realised that this dilapidated old pub facing the sea would make the most desirable residence if creativity and plenty of money were applied.

He, Jeremy had the latter and he could afford to hire someone who had the former - perfect.

Jeremy chuckled to himself all the way back on the train at the deal he had managed to pull off. The old guy didn't seem to want to close a deal at all and had made vague references to previous buyers not staying long in the area.

As this was to be a holiday home for him and Sabrina, an engagement gift once he had actually 'popped' the question, then staying long wasn't really an issue.

He just needed to convince her that he did intend to take breaks away from his business once he had a reliable manager in place. Whisking her off to the seaside every now and again would do the trick nicely.

Many phone calls, bank transfers and cheques later, the building was ready for furniture. Jeremy hadn't realised how much workmen still relied on cheques and no matter how he had tried to persuade them to join the 21st century, he could not.

The lack of speed shown in making the building presentable and the excuses about not working after dark because of the ghost stories they had heard, nearly drove him to distraction but his employee, James, who had managed the project, took most of the stress.

At least they had managed to employ builders from the neighbouring towns which helped time wise but Jeremy couldn't understand how no-one from the local village would be interested in the work.

He was a business man and he was happy to pay them cash in hand which surely would have helped their meagre little lives up here in the middle of nowhere.

Yes, the village was pretty and he was sure Sabrina would love it but the work opportunities couldn't be as overwhelming as the local craftsmen made out. Even James was twittering toward the end about perhaps finding somewhere less isolated.

James never directly admitted it was the local gossip stories that were concerning him, so he capitulated when Jeremy reminded him that the isolation was the point!

Fortunately, or perhaps unfortunately, depending on who's point of view you take, Jeremy decided to be in situ when the furniture arrived. He wanted to add the personal touch before Sabrina joined him for their first weekend at the 'cottage'. The latter was the only description he had given her, she had no idea what it was like or even where in the country it was.

It was only when he arrived at the coast that he got the call to say that the shop would not be delivering until the next day. He was annoyed but decided to buy a sleeping bag and a bottle of red wine and spend the night in his new acquisition rather than in a local B & B.

Just as it was turning dark Jeremy heard a strange creaking noise, he looked out of the bedroom window and there above him was the skull and crossbones swaying in the breeze.

He vaguely remembered James saying he couldn't get anyone to venture out to take down the old sign. Wimps! He would have a go himself first thing in the morning.

The lack of curtains wasn't really a problem as the moonlight was intermittent because of the clouds in the sky. The floor was the only wardrobe he needed for one night.

The wine was good and although the sleeping bag wasn't the most comfortable thing in the world, he felt relaxed, he laid back and fell asleep.

The squeaking noise continued and got louder – blasted sign! Ignore it – by this time tomorrow it would be in the scrap yard.

Whoosh! Jeremy felt something whiz past his ear, he turned his head. Whoosh! Now the other ear. What the! The sleeping bag seemed to be rising from the floor – it was a weird sensation.

Jeremy opened his eyes to find the bag was not moving at all and when he lifted his right arm out, it touched the floor. He had obviously been dreaming. He closed his eyes and went back to sleep.

The moaning and groaning sounds were fairly quite at first.

By the time Jeremy had realised what had woken him, it had reached fever pitch and again he got the sensation the sleeping bag was moving.

He wriggled to get his arms free and tried to get out but the zip was stuck, he tried to stand up but he fell over.

As he rolled round the floor trying desperately to get upright, the moaning and groaning was so loud he had to cover his ears.

The action caused the bag to slide down his body and without further thought he lunged forward, grabbed his pants, shoes and wallet and made his way out as if the devil himself was chasing him.

He would never be seen in the village again.

The old laggards were pleased with their night's work.

It actually was the most fun they had for a very long time not that they were into fun you understand.

Amazing how many people did not believe in ghosts and even more amazing how easy it was to convince them they were wrong! They returned to the cellar to the peace and familiarity they enjoyed.

Whether Belle was aware of the power of 'the others' to remove those who were in their way, was irrelevant as it had no impact on her existence.

However, that was about to change……

Chapter 7

There was a lot of movement in the main square but Belle ignored it as usual. Her attention was caught by something that looked a bit like her projection. Not as pretty or as nicely dressed but similar all the same.

Belle had watched others who lived in the solid structures before but this was different. They had always looked 'through' her and had never acknowledged her existence – she was used to that.

This image looked straight at her, smiled and waved. This was unusual. The image patted the space next to her and Belle approached the scene very slowly which again was unusual.

The image smiled again and included Belle in the make believe 'tea party' she was holding on the large stone seat that gave a beautiful view of the sea. Belle could do make believe!

Once all the furniture had been unloaded and the removal van was pulling away, a large image appeared in the doorway of the corner building and beckoned to them to join it.

The smaller image turned, smiled at Belle again and moved inside. Belle followed.

The moon was peeping through the clouds and the Old Jolly Rodger sign was swaying gently in the breeze outside the main bedroom window.

The creaking noise became louder and louder but did not manage to disturb the deaf couple in the double bed. They slept on, worn out by the day's activities.

The sensation of the bed moving or tipping did nothing except maybe increase their hold on slumber. The noise in the room reached a crescendo – Nothing!

No movement at all from the bed.

The mixture of old cantankerous sailors and pirates were confused – this had not happened before – they had always managed to move 'squatters' within a very short space of time.

It had to be said that these were the quietest interlopers they had ever encountered.

Normally music, shouting and laughter would alert them to the presence of unwanted guests. This time it was more of a sense of presence and the movement of furniture that had made them aware.

They decided to try again but despite some blood curdling sounds that any self-respecting ghost would be proud of, there was no response from the bed.

They looked at one another and their eyes glinted with an idea. The other bedroom – was anyone more susceptible in there?

They moved through the wall and there in the single bed in front of them was a little girl fast asleep but what they saw next stopped them in their tracks. They heard the tinkling noise at exactly the same time.

Belle was perched next to the child and was smiling at them. Not in a malicious way nor with any fear, just pure happiness. They had never seen her 'attached' to anything or anyone before – she was free as a bird usually.

Some at the back, who had not witnessed what those at the front has seen, started to make noises but again, like the adults, the child didn't move.

They moved forward ready to intimidate Belle and to try their movement sensation on the bed.

Belle didn't move, but the child did, her eyes opened as if she 'sensed' others in the room, she sat up in alarm and turned toward Belle who smiled at her sweetly and calmly.

The child returned the smile and settled back down to sleep.

Belle smiled at 'the others' in the room but did not move. They had never seen her still for that long.

They were confused again. They should be cross.

They should want to continue to make life difficult for these people who refused to show any interest in them.

They ought to be angry with Belle for interfering in their domain – who did she think she was?

They did not feel any of those things.

As they looked at Belle lying next to someone who it seemed she could relate to at last and be with whenever she wanted to be, the main emotion they felt was pride.

They were proud of her – they were proud of their village – she made it unique - no other Bay had a Beauty like Belle.

THE END

42850231R00025

Printed in Poland
by Amazon Fulfillment
Poland Sp. z o.o., Wrocław